Comet

Vomit

COMET VOMIT

Dyan Blacklock

ORCHARD BOOKS

For Frances Horrocks,
my mother

ORCHARD BOOKS
96 Leonard Street, London EC2A 4RH
Orchard Books Australia
14 Mars Road, Lane Cove, NSW 2066
ISBN 1 86039 252 0 (hardback)
ISBN 1 86039 267 9 (paperback)
Originally published in Australia 1995
by Allen and Unwin Pty Ltd
First published in Great Britain 1996
First paperback publication 1996
Text copyright © Dyan Blacklock 1995
A CIP catalogue record for this book is available from the British Library.
Printed in Great Britain

CONTENTS

COMET VOMIT

Friday 13 May was the night of the annual Miss Yabbie Ball in Bonnandarry, which was why a spaceship was able to land practically unobserved in Frenchman's Field.

Old Mrs Phillips saw it, but since no one ever believed her anyway she never mentioned it. The captain of a Boeing 727 saw it, too, but he had a wife and three children to support, so he never said anything either. The only other person who saw the saucer land was Tyrone Dalgleish.

At the time the spacecraft began to hover over the field, Tyrone was pulling up two nets he had set in Mr McGuire's dam, where Mr McGuire had hundreds of his biggest and best yabbies, all fat and happy and ready to breed. It gave Tyrone a terrible fright to look up and see hot white lights across the field. At first he thought it was the police, come to arrest him for nicking Mr McGuire's yabbies, and he had thrown the nets to the bottom of the dam before he realised it was a spaceship.

The thing made no noise at all when it landed. As soon as it settled, the lights went out. There was complete silence, and Tyrone couldn't even see it any more. He slid down the dam wall and bellied across the paddock, stopping about a metre from where he thought it had landed. Cautiously he stood up—and whacked his skull so hard on the bottom of the ship that for a moment his eyes rolled around in his head. He sat down with a thump and looked up. There was nothing but the sky above him, the black starless sky, and the outlines of ghost gums. Reaching up, his fingertips felt something very cold and smooth. He traced the curved outline of the hull upwards from where he crouched until he could stand alongside it.

Then Tyrone remembered his nets were in the bottom of the dam and there was no chance he could fish them out again. It had taken him two weeks to make those nets. He cursed out loud and thumped his fist on the side of the invisible spaceship. As soon as he hit the metal, a humming sound filled his head and a thin sliver of light appeared. He stopped swearing and peered up.

'Tyrone Dalgleish?' a voice said.

Tyrone knew better than to talk to strange spaceships. He shut his mouth and waited.

'We have been watching you,' the voice went on. 'This is the third time you have been observed taking yabbies from this dam.'

'Wrong,' Tyrone blurted out. 'I didn't get any this time, thanks to you.'

The spaceship was silent.

'Anyway, Mr McGuire's got more than he needs. He's never gunna miss the few I get.' Tyrone began to feel annoyed. It was one thing to lose his nets because a blinding light popped up out of the blue; it was another to be told off for poaching a few yabbies.

'I hope you realise I dropped both my nets in that dam when you shone your headlights in my face,' he whined. 'I think you oughta fish them out again for me. That can't be too hard for an advanced civilisation like yours.'

There was a gasp from inside the spaceship. The voice boomed out over Tyrone's head: 'Take heed, Dalgleish, we will not tolerate such environmental vandalism. We will not return your weapons to you.'

'Weapons?' Tyrone was interested but confused. 'Who said anything about weapons? I'm talking about my nets.'

'And so are we.' The voice sounded icy. 'These nets are nothing but weapons. What they catch, you—Dalgleish—kill. You are an environmental criminal. You can be arrested and tried for your crimes.' The space voice sounded smug.

'Oh yeah?' Tyrone bristled. 'I suppose you realise you're on private property right now and that you just killed at least a thousand bugs when you landed?'

Another gasp from inside the spaceship. 'We are the Stellar Command Ship *The Guardian*.' The voice faltered. 'We have no choice but to take out a few of the lower forms of life as we land. Everyone knows it happens. Sometimes we get a human or a kangaroo or some big thing that just won't get out of the way in time, but we don't make a point of it. Accidents happen.'

Tyrone knew he was on a roll. 'Good one, Dr Spock. You can squash a kangaroo or make mincemeat out of Uncle Freddy, but I can't catch a few fat yabbies.' He started to walk back towards the dam. 'Just you try to arrest me. I bet you've got no warrant.'

The light grew brighter over his head and the voice began to snigger.

'Sorry, Dalgleish, we don't need a warrant. This is an interstellar space probe for universal animal rights. We have lasercuffs and hurlwalls. We have automatic stun darts and thinksters that can reprogram you in a second. You're sprung, kid.' There was a mad giggle from somewhere above Tyrone's head.

'Old hat!' Tyrone shouted back. 'That stuff went out with the ark. Where are you from, anyway, the outer suburbs of space? I've got toys that can do more than that on one battery.'

A gurgling noise came out of the air.

'Dalgleish, you have to atone for your crimes against the environment. We are here to save the yabby from predators such as yourself.'

'Well, that's a laugh.' Tyrone pointed to the dam. 'Mr McGuire breeds his yabbies for the restaurant trade in Sydney. He sells them by the kilo, and I just get a dozen every now and again for Mum. You people should get your facts straight. If the universe is relying on space police like you, then it's got a problem. I've a good mind to report you for interfering with my business and making me drop my nets in the dam.' He folded his arms over his chest and stared at the light above him. 'And while I'm at it, I might make an official complaint of environmental harassment.'

'What?' the voice choked. 'You can't do that.'

'I wouldn't make a bet on it, rivet body. I have my rights, you know.'

The voice wheedled, 'No need to be hasty, Mr Dalgleish, we can talk about this like two grown furds.'

'Like two grown *what*?' Tyrone put both hands on his hips and stuck his face up at the light. 'Get this straight, you lump of space debris, you are not talking to some dumb furd.' He wondered for a moment what a furd looked like. 'I want your patrol number, mister.'

There was a brief silence as the voice took stock. When it spoke again it sounded silky and smooth. 'We have reviewed the facts of your case, Mr Dalgleish, and it seems our computer has made a slight error. We apologise for the inconvenience.'

'Never mind apologising, hydrogen breath, I want my nets back, and I want them back before you go, or I'm getting in touch with your superior.'

There were sounds of scuffling and scraping from inside the ship. A long thin silver rod slid out of the midnight air and hovered over the dam. A fine iridescent line with a shining hook dropped into the water. The rod dipped and dragged across the surface and caught on something. A neat flick threw the first of Tyrone's nets on the dam wall, the other followed close behind.

'You've got fishing rods!' Tyrone was amazed.

'There's no need to shout,' the voice whispered.

'You're not supposed to have fishing rods,' Tyrone was sure of that.

'We could come to some arrangement about this.' The voice sounded flustered.

'Like what, comet vomit?' Tyrone was thinking fast. 'Maybe if you leave that fishing rod with me, I could forget I ever saw you. I could tear up my complaint and you furds could be on your way.' He smiled slyly. 'I'm not unreasonable.'

The rod floated silently to the ground. Tyrone picked it up. 'Thanks a lot.' He turned it over in his hands. 'Nice one, Furdy. Tell you what, why don't you keep one of my nets?' He lifted a net up on the end of the rod. 'I think I'll go over to Hardy's dam. Trout would make a nice change from yabbies.'

Tyrone distinctly heard the sound of lips smacking together. 'Mr Dalgleish?'

'Yes, Furdo?'

'What exactly do yabbies taste like?'

SHARK BAIT

Harry Lord sat down with a thud. His new Reeboks were covered in red dirt; his legs below the knees were covered in rivulets of sweat and blood.

'This is stupid,' he shouted, 'bloody stupid. This lantana's gunna rip my face off in a minute. It's right over my head. I can't see a thing.' He punched at the bush, a wild angry swipe that tore his knuckles on the thorny tangle of lantana above him. Dead leaves rained down, covering him in fine debris. His breathing became more laboured. 'It's giving me bloody asthma.' He shook out his shirt to get rid of the lantana leaves and scrabbled in his shorts for his puffer. His soft mouth covered the Ventolin inhaler and he shot three squirts deep into his throat.

'Oahh, I hate this stuff.'

'The Ventolin?' His mate Andrew cleared a small space in the dirt and sat down alongside him.

'Jeez you're stupid sometimes. I mean I hate this dumb climbing through the bush on some idiot adventure. I dunno why I let you talk me into it every time. You're always dragging me off into the bloody bush and making me go down twenty-metre cliffs just to see some stone or weed or—'

'Fish.' Andrew finished the sentence for him. 'We're going to see fish.'

Harry sighed. His breathing was easier now. He wiped at his legs and smeared the sticky red mess even further across his skin. 'These scratches'll probably get infected.' He peered at his legs. Already the skin was puffy and angry-looking around the cuts. 'How far till we get to the water? We've been going for ages, and I still can't see anything that looks like an estuary.'

Andrew gestured vaguely with his hand. 'Just down there,' he said. 'The lantana runs out just above the high-water mark, and the mangroves take over. We're going across the slope till we get under the bridge, then we'll drop down to the water. We can sit right under the bridge. There's a flat rock that sticks out. You can chuck stuff at the pylon from it.'

'*You* might be able to,' Harry said, 'You know I can't throw for peanuts.'

'It's easy. I'll show you how. Come on. About another ten minutes and we'll be there.'

'Yeah, and then when we get there we have to come back through all this again.' Harry dug his heels in. 'I don't wanna go.'

'Look,' Andrew spoke slowly, 'I was going to save this for when we got down there, but I'll tell you a bit now.' He paused. 'There was a boy eaten by a giant shark down there once.'

'Bull!'

'No bull. Eaten alive, right next to the pylon.'

'Go on, tell me.' Harry was interested. The thought of another boy being taken by a huge shark filled him with a heady mix of dread and pleasure.

'When we get there.'

Andrew had him, he knew. Harry loved a good story.

'It better not be too far,' Harry grumbled as he got to his feet. 'If we're not there in ten minutes, I'm going back.'

They pushed on in single file, with Andrew leading the way. Every step was treacherous as they wound their way across the steep bank that sloped into the water, still invisible because of the jungle of bushes surrounding them. Slipping and sliding on patches of bare dirt, crashing through thickets of lantana, they shouted and swore and laughed. The sharp outcrops of rock became more pronounced. In places oyster shells stuck out like jagged razors, ready to slash their shins if they fell. Tumbling and hooting they burst clear of the bush onto a long narrow platform of sandstone that jutted out into the water. It was pitted with shallow depressions forming tidal pools, each one brimming with life. Tiny orange-backed crabs scurried sideways as fast as they could to escape this wild invasion of boys.

Harry grabbed one and flung it into the water. 'Can't get me, crabbie, I'm too fast!' He searched at his feet for another. 'We shoulda brought a bucket. This stuff'd make great bait.'

Andrew lay prone on the rock, his face a few inches from the water, his fingers curling over the edge. 'No point. We're not going to catch fish, we're going to look at them.'

'It's black as pitch down there,' Harry complained. 'How can we see anything?'

'You have to lie down like this and get real close to it, then you can see heaps.'

'I wanna chuck stuff. You said you'd show me. Come on, we can look at the fish later.' Harry cast around for something to throw. A few small rocks went flying across the estuary.

'I need something heavier,' he whined. 'These are too light.'

'Have a look in the bush over there,' Andrew suggested. 'There's probably bigger stuff up higher.'

Harry searched the nearby scrub. 'Hey, Andrew, how about this?' He held aloft a shoe, its dusty black leather cracking and splitting with age. 'Musta been here for ages, it looks ancient.'

Andrew turned to look. His eyes lit up and he sucked in his breath. 'Do you know what you've got there? You've got *his* shoe. I bet that's the very shoe he took off before he went swimming.'

'Who?'

'The kid who got eaten here. It was years ago, and it happened right here next to this rock.' He spoke in a reverential whisper. 'Right here, Harry. He took off his shoes and jumped in.'

'Did he take off his clothes, too? He musta taken off his clothes, right?'

'His clothes have rotted away to nothing by now.

There's just that shoe left.' Andrew felt the mystery and fear pulse through him. 'He came down here one afternoon in January, just him and a mate.'

'Like us!' Harry interrupted.

'Yeah, like us. It was just about this time. Late afternoon. They decided to cool off, so he stripped and jumped in.'

'Then the shark got him!' Harry shivered with the thrill of it.

'Not straight away, it didn't.' Andrew paused. 'He swam about ten metres out, over there under the pylon. He was shouting and splashing, calling for his mate to jump in.'

'Did he? Jump in too, I mean.'

'No, he needed a leak, so he took one off the rock before he got in.'

'Like this!' Harry stood up and unzipped his fly. He shot a jet of pee far into the water. 'Does this bring sharks? Is that what happened?'

'Dogs, blood and pee—they all attract sharks.'

'Was there a dog too?' Harry wished they'd brought a dog with them.

'Yeah, there was a dog. A red setter. It loved the water. It jumped in with him.' Andrew ran his hand through the green water. 'He never saw the shark before it hit him. It was a tiger shark, about five metres long, all brown and smooth and full of teeth. It must have just spawned up in the mangroves and been on its way out to sea. It would have been hungry.'

'Hungry enough to eat him?'

'Yeah, hungry enough to rip him in two and swallow half in one piece. His mate saw it happen from here.'

'Jeez! I'd be sick.'

'He was. He threw up for days afterwards. He had to run back up there to the road and get help, chucking all the way.'

'Wow!' Harry sat down on the edge of the rock. He splashed water over his legs and washed the deep scratches with salt water. They stung, making him think of bodies being torn apart. 'Then what happened?'

'The police came back down. They couldn't find even a tiny bit of him, just bloody foam at the edge of the rock.' Andrew was silent for a moment.

Harry picked up the shoe and held it over his head. 'We should chuck his shoe in. Sort of a burial service.'

As he drew his shoulder back and lunged forward to throw the shoe, his body followed in a wild overbalancing arc. Andrew grabbed Harry by the shorts and pulled him back. The shoe fell short of the throw, plopping into the murky water directly in front of them.

'That was close.' They both laughed.

The shoe floated for a moment a few inches from the rock, a black bobbing shape slowly filling with water as they watched, mesmerised. Then, from out of the depths, a giant torpedo shape, all brown and smooth and full of teeth, slid silently forward. Its huge jaws gaped open and swallowed the shoe in one lazy bite. It sank again before they were even sure what they had seen.

It was Andrew who spoke first. 'Jeez,' he said in a whisper. 'It came back for the shoe!'

No Galaxy too Small

Cameron was talking to himself and pulling faces in the mirror. His sister Judith snapped her book shut and looked at him.

'You are abnormal, are you aware of that? If enough people ever find out how truly weird you are, then you'll probably be locked up for ever.'

'I hate you too.'

'Just don't come out of this room while my friends are here.'

'Your friends stink. And they're ugly, like you. How much do you have to pay them?'

'Pathetic, Cameron. Truly pathetic.' Judith gave her brother a withering look. 'You are not capable of an original thought. There's no way you are ever going to be any smarter than you are right now. How tragic.' She gave the little laugh that Cameron hated most of all and walked out, pulling the door shut. His room was wall-to-wall with her clothes. He hated it when she came home on holidays from boarding school.

'Why doesn't Mum make her stay there all year long?' he muttered and threw himself at the bed. 'It's great when she's not here.'

His mother burst through the door carrying an armful of folded washing.

'Cameron, I want you to clean up this pigsty, now!' Whenever she was in a foul mood she came and shouted at him to clean his room. 'I see no reason whatever for your room to be kept like this.'

Cameron sat up. 'None of this is my mess. Why don't you ever shout at Judith?'

'I don't shout at her because she is fifteen and she is also responsible.'

'I'm responsible!'

'You're eleven, you are a long way from being responsible, Cameron. If you were responsible then this room wouldn't look like this.' She began to push bundles of clothes into the too-small drawers in his too-small wardrobe.

'I can never get anything out of there after you put the washing away.' He threw his sister's discarded clothes onto her bed. His mother spun around. 'Bad move,' he thought to himself, but it was too late: she threw the last of the washing at his chest.

'You put the clothes away then, smart alec. And don't leave this room until it's tidy.' She slammed the door shut behind her.

Cameron dropped the neatly-folded washing onto the floor and kicked it savagely. 'Don't come out till it's clean; don't come out till you're normal,' he mimicked his mother and sister in a high sing-song voice. Then he dropped to his knees and wrung his hands together, pretending to sob loudly. 'Oh, please, whoever's in charge of smelly, abnormal boys; make me normal, make me clean!'

He shuffled over the washing to the mirror and had just made a really grotesque face and was concentrating on getting his top lip to roll all the way back from his teeth when the door opened and a small moon-faced person stepped quietly into the room. He had on a gold uniform that made Cameron think of parades and pageants. His hands, which were huge, smoothed at the fabric of his jacket.

'I think we should begin by ceasing to make weird faces in the mirror, Cameron,' the intruder said in a soft voice. 'It's one of the abnormal behaviours we at the URS like to eradicate first.'

Cameron sat back on his feet and stared with his mouth open. A small trickle of saliva, the result of so much lip-stretching, ran down his chin in a most unattractive way.

'Dribble on the chin is considered both abnormal *and* unclean, Cameron.'

Cameron wiped his chin with the back of his hand and dried it on his jeans. He was speechless with surprise.

'I don't think you called for me a moment too soon, I can see there is a *lot* to be done.' The moon face puckered into a small wrinkle of distaste. A long, knobbly finger pointed at the floor under Cameron's bed.

'There are twelve pairs of old underpants under your bed, Cameron. Put them in this plastic bag and take them to the laundry.' The knobbly fingers held out a bright yellow plastic bag.

'Generally speaking you will use yellow bags for all contaminants which must be destroyed, and blue for those which can be recycled in some way. I left in such a rush I didn't have time to get the blue bags. There is a bowl of congealed noodles on the windowsill right there, alongside the chocolate cake crumbs. Articles of this nature will require both bags.'

Moon-face had begun to hover a few centimetres above the floor. 'It will be necessary to vacuum this floor immediately; I find I have stepped in something unspeakable.'

Cameron tried to make a sound but couldn't manage anything more than a kind of grunting noise.

'Until such time as you think before you speak, and then speak intelligently, I am afraid I have suspended your voice rights.'

'Mggleoink!' Cameron choked with anger.

'Perhaps a quick peek at the future will help to convince you.' Moon-face clicked a tiny green control in his belt. A large screen appeared on the bedroom wall and Cameron recognised himself, a lot older and with real muscles and facial hair, but otherwise unmistakably himself. 'Note, if you will, the effect your passing by has on the other people in the street.'

The other Cameron was walking down a busy city street. Nearly everyone he passed stepped out wide as they reached him, and held their noses.

'This is the result of failing to take a bath for eleven

weeks, and not having brushed your teeth at all for six months.' Moon-face pressed the green control again and another picture appeared on the screen. It was a close-up of the teeth in the other Cameron's mouth. They were greenish and all the cracks were filled to the brim with food scraps. A dark stain was beginning to spread across them. 'Most of your teeth have decayed to the point where they will need to be removed.' A dentist's drill started to whine loudly.

Cameron shuddered.

'This is your fiftieth birthday party.' The screen flashed again and there was Cameron, a lot older and with grey hair, standing toothless and alone in a small dirty room, holding a paper cup of Coke and singing happy birthday to himself. 'Not a pretty sight.' Moon-face adjusted the long row of gold medals across his chest. He flicked the switch on his belt.

The screen vanished and Cameron gulped loudly. 'Urf-fleoink,' he grunted. 'Mrrglumph wooglerrg bufflloink.'

Moon-face nodded sympathetically. 'Quite so, my boy. You have no friends. Those who were not repulsed by your lack of personal hygiene have been either insulted or bored to death by you. I'm sorry, but as you can see, there is no time to lose. We must begin today to make you clean and normal.' He smiled. 'You're very lucky to have me as your facilitator. I have a number of awards in this area already.' He patted his medals.

Cameron groaned. For the next two hours he cleaned his room. It felt like being on an archaeological dig; he unearthed months of debris from corners, and under or behind furniture. Enough to fill four yellow bags.

'Phroopyglk?' He looked pleadingly at Moon-face.

'Very well, I will return your voice rights for the time being, you've done a splendid job!' Cameron beamed, then frowned. He tried his voice cautiously. 'Are . you . an . alien?'

'Very intelligent, well done. I am indeed an alien. I am the fourteenth highest ranking employee of the Universal Rehabilitation Service. "No galaxy too small" is our motto. We are constantly on the go, rehabilitating eleven-year-old boys throughout the universe.'

'What about girls?' Cameron demanded. 'What about fifteen-year-old girls?'

'In some very severe cases we occasionally move fifteen-year-old girls to a minor star in the Andromeda galaxy for more permanent reprogramming,' Moon-face said. 'But we find girls have to be rehabilitated much earlier.

By fifteen the damage has been done. There's a separate unit that deals with nine-year-old girls.'

'That's unfair. Why didn't someone fix Judith when she was nine? Now she'll be like this forever and I have to share my room with her every four months when she comes home on holiday!'

'She didn't ask.' Moon-face looked surprised. 'The client must ask for help, like you did.'

'I was only joking about that. I didn't really mean it.'

'We at the URS do not differentiate between joking and non-joking requests. Once you ask, we come. Once we come, you begin rehabilitation. It is that simple.'

Cameron began to be truly afraid. 'How long does it take, usually I mean?'

'That varies. In some cases, a week is long enough. In your case, it is likely I will be here for six months.' Moon-face smiled. 'You had better get used to me, I am here for the long haul.'

Judith screamed as her brother sat down to breakfast. 'Aarggh! Help! Mum, Cameron's clean! Quick! Get a photograph of him now before he turns into a dirt ball again.'

His mother ruffled his hair affectionately. 'He's growing up, Judith. That's all. It happens to all boys eventually.'

Cameron smiled at his mother and ate his cereal neatly. He washed his plate and dried his hands on the hand-towel, put his homework into his bag along with the sandwich he'd made, and headed for the bathroom to brush his teeth.

Moon-face was sitting on the edge of the bath. He looked very pleased with himself.

'Well, Cameron, I think we may be finished here. You have really been an excellent student. I didn't think we'd get it all done in four short months, but there you are. You have been something of a star case in the URS, you know. My superiors are very impressed. Actually, I'm in line for a promotion because of you.' Moon-face almost smirked.

'Really?' Cameron looked up slyly. 'Better pay and conditions I suppose?'

'Oh indeed. I shall be tenth-ranking officer on the Pleasure Cruiser, Red Star. It's a *very* good job.'

'Hmm.' Cameron stopped brushing his teeth. 'And it's all because of my rapid rehabilitation, you say?'

'I *am* known for my abilities in this area.' Moon-face

squared his shoulders and the medals shone. 'There's always a way, I always say!'

Cameron began to smile. Slowly and deliberately he squeezed a little toothpaste out of the tube and onto his shirt front. He rubbed the bristles of his sister's toothbrush deep into the soap. Moon-face frowned.

'We dealt with bathroom behaviour in the first month, Cameron. Really!'

Cameron filled the sink with hot water and dropped the soap to the bottom. He looked Moon-face in the eye.

'You're right,' he said. 'There's always a way. As a matter of fact, I think it's time we had a little chat about exactly what I get out of all this.' Tug, tug, tug. All the towels lay on the floor in a heap.

Moon-face knew what was coming.

'It's always the same with eleven-year-old boys,' he muttered. His lips trembled. 'I've had to work very hard for these.' The medals jangled.

Cameron sprinkled talcum powder over the wet bench.

'I don't want much,' he said, reasonably. He poured his sister's shampoo over the talc. Moon-face could see the Red Star departing without him. 'In fact, it's Judith who wants something. Remember that planet where they send really severe cases of fifteen-year-old girls?'

Moon-face nodded morosely.

'Well, I heard Judith ask for help this morning. She really wants to go!'

His sister began to hammer on the bathroom door. 'You're talking to yourself again, Cameron. Get out of there you little nose-pick. I want to brush my teeth.'

Moon-face sighed. 'Would three years be long enough?'

'Let's just review it in three years, shall we?' Cameron opened the bathroom door.

'Judith, I'd like you to meet a friend of mine.'

SURFING THE WHEAT

From here to there a blue haze shivered across the flat, flat plains of wheat. There was not even a bush to interrupt the endless thin horizon.

Dudley Budd shifted his shorts so they stopped pinching his leg. He flicked away a fly, and scratched his cheek. Huge freckles dotted his skin like spots of mud. He shaded his pale eyes with his hand as he squinted into the distance, watching the blue and yellow landscape intently. A hawk hovered above the wheat, then dropped silently, invisible for a moment then rising again with something in its talons.

Dudley brushed the red dust off the stones at his feet. His fingers closed over a perfect flat, round rock. He tucked it in between his finger and thumb and sent it spinning across the top of the wheat, touching the very tips and arcing high above the field before it plummeted to the ground. The wheat closed over it like water. He wished he was somewhere else. It was all he could think of since his American cousins had stayed.

'Boy.' They had sat together where he sat now. 'This place is beautiful.'

'What's so great about One Tree Flat?' Dudley looked around him. The place was a dust bowl. 'There isn't even a truck stop in town where you can buy a hamburger.'

'That's just it. There's nothing but the sky and the wheat and the birds. No billboards, no traffic. Just this wide open space. You don't know how lucky you are.'

Dudley stared at them. He tried to imagine Hawaii, but he couldn't.

'There's nothing like this back home.'

'Duuud-llley!' His mother's voice brought him to his feet. He shoved his hands into his pockets and walked towards the railway line. Dudley was in no hurry; whatever Mum wanted would wait; nothing happened fast at One Tree Flat. He dawdled across the paddock. A light gust of wind raked the wheat near him and sent a wave through the whole field. It rippled and swayed as the wind swept along through the tall yellow grass.

He pushed the wire screen door with his foot and it banged shut behind him; a small cloud of dust rose and fell at the step.

'Dudley.'

'Yes, Mum?'

'Bill Irvine brought something for you just now on the back of his ute.'

His mother poked her finger at the back door. Leaning up against the verandah was a surfboard.

'There's a letter with it, Dud.' His mother pushed a thick envelope into his hands. 'From your cousins in Hawaii.'

He opened it. Inside was a long red plastic wallet and a sheet of airmail paper.

'What's it say, Dud?'

He began to read.

'Thank you for the best holiday of our lives. Hawaii feels like one huge shopping mall since we came back. We thought a lot about what to send you. We wanted you to have something no one else in One Tree Flat would ever have, so in the end we decided on this surfboard.'

He stopped reading and flung the letter onto the table. 'What am I ever gunna do with a surfboard, Mum?' How could his cousins have been so dumb?

His mother picked up the letter and read on.

'You're so lucky to have those wheat fields. It's like an ocean out there, always changing and moving. There's nothing like it in Hawaii.'

His mother looked out the window at the paddocks of grain. 'You know, Dud, I sometimes think that too; it is like the ocean.' She read on. 'In case you decide you'd like the kind of surf that gets you wet, enclosed is one ticket to Hawaii.'

Dudley looked up.

'Are you kidding?'

She pushed the red plastic folder across at him. 'No, Dud, there's a ticket here all right.'

He stared at the travel folder as she pulled out a ticket, traveller's cheques and a picture of Hawaii.

'It's for the Christmas holidays,' she said slowly, a smile spreading across her face. 'You think you'd like to go?'

He looked out over the plains. In the late afternoon light they were a warm gold, wave upon wave. Dudley felt a sudden sense of belonging.

'It depends,' he said.

'On what, Dud?'

'Well,' he said slowly, and grinned. 'It depends on whether the surf's up in the wheat fields at Christmas.'

FROG GUTS

It wasn't my idea to cut a frog open. Mrs Rattsoff made me do it.

'Does everyone have their frog?'

'Yes Mrs Rattsoff.'

Ever notice how thirty kids sound like one loud person?

'In a minute I will ask you to put your frog in the bell jar on the bench in front of you.'

I know what a bell jar is; it's a big glass dome for killing small animals.

'You will all see that inside your bell jar is a piece of cottonwool.'

Like we're blind or something. Rattsoff always tells us the things we can figure out ourselves, and *still* think about last night's TV.

'Now who can tell me what the cottonwool is for?'

Maybe it's for sticking in your ears so you won't hear the rest of this lesson. I don't say that, but I'd like to. Instead someone pipes up, 'It's to make the frog go to sleep, Mrs Rattsoff.'

Some sleep. Better not try to wake up. Your little froggy guts will be all spilled out on the dissecting board. Maybe my frog is thinking right now: this is all a dream, in a minute I'm going to wake up safe and sound back in my own little pond. Fat chance, frog. You're going to that great pond in the sky to join the million other frogs who've been chopped open in the name of science.

'You will put ten drops of chloroform on the cottonwool from the bottle in front of you. This will put the frog to sleep painlessly.'

How does she know what's painless for a frog? I bet it'll wish it had taken a holiday in Queensland this year instead of hopping into the net. Who caught this frog anyway? What kind of person has a job catching frogs all day long for kids to dissect? I hope it pays well.

'It will take about five minutes for the frog to be completely dead.'

Does she think the frog could be partly dead? It's either

dead or it's not. Then again, Mrs Rattsoff looks partly dead. Her skin is the colour of the old white sheets that Dad uses when he's painting the house. Some of her hairs are grey. She's forty, easy.

'Your frog has not been fed for the last twenty-four hours; this will help the chloroform to do its job more rapidly. When we examine the stomach contents you will see that most of the food will have passed through and into the intestine.'

Science is after lunch. I reckon Rattsoff must bolt her food. She's always choking down burps when she talks. I bet if you examined her stomach contents today you'd find a salami and onion sandwich floating around down there.

'Now, one partner will drop the chloroform onto the cottonwool, and the other will please remove the frog from its container and place it under the bell jar.'

Which one should I do? I don't want to be the one who sticks froggy into the death chamber, and I don't want to be the one who drops the death gas on the cottonwool. I could just argue about this with my partner for a while, and let our frog escape while we talk. Run, frog! Back to the pond, back to the forest! Back to the end of the science lab is more likely. Poor frog will end up getting chased to death by thirty morons with chloro-form balls.

I decide to drop the death gas. I won't use ten drops. That's too awful. I'll just put in a couple of drops. It's only a tiny little frog. It can't take too much chloroform to make it die.

My partner sticks our soft brown frog into the gas chamber. Frog has a smile on its face. It doesn't know that this is the end.

'Watch your frog carefully to see that all signs of life are extinguished before you remove the bell jar.' Burp. Mrs Rattsoff starts to walk around the lab to check if all the little frogs are going to sleep.

'Make sure the bell jar is on properly; see that there are no gaps.'

I look. There are no gaps to let the death gas escape. I go like my death gas is getting me. 'Aargh. Death gas!' I pretend to choke, clutch my throat. My partner thinks it's for real. Mrs Rattsoff flicks my head with her finger.

'Oww!' That really hurts.

'Now, remove your frog and place it on the wooden board in front of you.'

My partner lifts froggy out, all limp and still.

'Stretch each limb and pin it to the board, belly side up.'

These thick pins go right through the feet and legs. I feel sick.

'When the frog is firmly secured to the board, take the scalpel in front of you, carefully remove the safety cover and make a slice through the skin from top to bottom, like this.' She draws a red line right down the middle of the frog diagram on the blackboard.

Suddenly my lunch is very close to my mouth. I can't do this, I can't watch. I want to bolt for the door.

'Are you all wearing your surgical gloves? Good. Examine the gut by pulling it out gently and slowly onto the board. Note particularly how long it is.'

My partner has no trouble with this. Guts start to ooze through the hole. I think I'm really going to faint.

'Now, if you pull the skin back at the top of the cut and look carefully, you will see the diaphragm. In a living animal it moves up and down as the creature breathes.'

Why is my froggy's diaphragm moving up and down?

'Behind the diaphragm lies the heart. When alive, it pulses.'

'Please, Mrs Rattsoff, this frog's heart is still beating.'

I am scared. I have not killed my frog. I have its guts on the table, and it's alive.

Rattsoff is nice about it. She looks and screams a bit and goes whiter than usual and doesn't even burp once.

'Sew it back up will you?' I plead with her. 'Stick its guts back in. Fix my frog.'

She doesn't, of course. I know she can't. Instead she puts more death gas on another piece of cottonwool and holds it over the frog's face. The rest of the class wants to see the heart beating, but Rattsoff won't let them.

It was okay in the end. I got to take the frog home and bury it in the backyard. Mrs Rattsoff thought it might make me feel better. Everyone wanted to sit with me on the bus going home.

I kept thinking about my diaphragm, with my heart behind it. Beating.

The Storm

The day had been hot and still. Now, at dusk, the bay was glassy.

Jeremy sat on the slimy water-washed steps that led from the end of the jetty into the deep green water. His chest felt tight. He made himself stay where he was for a few more minutes.

At North Head a summer storm was building. The late afternoon light glowed orange through the bulging, blue-grey thunderhead. Jeremy shivered uncontrollably. His T-shirt felt skimpy, and his legs were suddenly cold. It was time to get back home and be inside. He got to his feet immediately. It would take him four minutes to run up the winding hill to his house, and when he got there he would be out of breath and gasping for air. If he was careful he could get to his room without anyone noticing him. Jeremy ran.

'I've organised fishing lessons for you both. They start today.'

His two sons sat still at the breakfast table.

'I've got drum practice today, Dad.' Tony jabbed his spoon into the cereal in a small defiant gesture, not lost on his father.

'I know. The fishing lesson is for this afternoon at dusk. It'll be great.' He looked from child to child, pleading silently with them to show some enthusiasm for his plan. 'When I was your age I caught a ten-kilo jewfish. Most exciting moment of my life.'

Jeremy sighed. A long, whispery sigh that escaped before he could stop it. He had heard this story before.

'I don't want any nonsense from you, Jeremy. It's about time you grew up. Fishing won't kill you.' The pleading look vanished completely.

'Yes, Dad.' Jeremy looked at his feet.

Tony stood up and pushed his chair hard against the table. 'I'll be back at four,' was all he said.

The low stone wall at the edge of the foreshore walk was almost empty when the two boys came down at dusk. Already lights were coming on in the big houses that fronted the beach. Jeremy tried not to look at the sky. He kept his face to the ground and walked steadily towards the jetty. Alongside him, Tony swung a small tackle box over his shoulder in reckless arcs.

'You'll be sorry if that thing flies open, Tony.'

'I hope it does. Then I'd have to spend the next two hours picking hooks off the footpath instead of catching disgusting fish.' He looked sharply at his brother. 'Anyway, you can't be too anxious to sit on a jetty fishing when there's a storm coming up.'

Jeremy forced himself to look at the path and not at the horizon. The effort of controlling his fear made a light sweat break out on his skin.

'Doesn't bother me. I'm not scared of storms any more.'

Tony shrugged. 'Have it your way, Jezza,' he said almost kindly. 'Look, that must be the guy over there.'

Leaning against the end of the jetty was a young man holding a swag of fishing rods. Two other boys were talking earnestly to him.

'Great!' Tony smiled broadly. 'A couple of eager fishermen. Just what the doctor ordered. Maybe they'll ask so many stupid fish questions we won't have to actually do any fishing.' He laughed, and Jeremy joined in.

'Don't worry, Jezza.' Tony gave his brother a gentle shove. 'It won't be for long. If I can put up with this, so can you.' Resolutely the two boys quickened their step.

The man with the fishing rods was called Ron. He turned to face the brothers as they approached across the sand.

'Good-oh!' He sounded cheerful. 'We're all here.'

Jeremy shuffled his feet in the warm white grains. He glanced quickly at the fisherman's face, and looked away just as swiftly. He saw a kind face, brown eyes and a stained windcheater.

The other boys were clearly eager to get on with it. Grasping their rods, buckets and tackle boxes they walked towards the rocks jutting out into the bay. A faraway rumble sounded across the water. Jeremy began to tremble.

'Aren't we going to fish off the jetty?' His voice shook.

'Not tonight. We're going off the rocks.' Ron looked more closely at him. 'It's perfectly safe. The tide won't change for another hour. We won't get washed off or anything.'

'Rock fishing is unsafe.' Tony stopped walking. 'I think we should fish off the jetty,' he said petulantly.

Ron stopped too.

'We could try fishing off the jetty, but the odds are we won't get so much as a nibble. The tide's too low for jetty fishing. The fish are all around the rocks at this time of night, feeding. That's where we'll hook up. Besides, these are harbour rocks, not an ocean platform.'

For a moment, no one moved.

'I'll keep my eye on you both, don't worry.' Ron picked up the rods and began to walk towards the rocks again. Reluctantly the brothers followed.

'This'll do nicely.' Ron laid the gear carefully on the low, sloping platform. 'First thing to do is rig up. You all know how to tie a blood knot?'

'I thought that's what you're supposed to be teaching us,' Tony muttered under his breath. The other boys were already tying expert knots and laughing in anticipation. Jeremy sat huddled against the sharp rock face, fear and misery etched on his features. The storm was gathering momentum in the night sky. Flashes of lightning lit the horizon from time to time, and deep rumbling thunder rolled across the bay.

'The storm worrying you?' Ron squatted in front of

him. 'These rods are fibreglass, not carbon graphite, you know.'

Jeremy wondered what on earth he was talking about.

'Lightning strikes.' Ron grinned. 'Less chance of them if you're holding fibreglass rods.'

The very idea filled Jeremy with panic. Even in the dark his face looked white.

'You and your brother aren't too keen on fishing, I take it?' Ron glanced over at Tony, struggling with the rod and tackle.

'I don't mind it.' Jeremy's breathing had become laboured. 'Tony hates it.'

'What's up with you then?'

'Nothing.'

'Going to fish?'

With an enormous effort, Jeremy stood up and walked to the rock edge. Tony was swearing loudly.

'How're you supposed to get a tiny little hook on in the bloody dark? Why can't we use a big hook I can see?'

'Big hooks catch big fish.' Ron's voice was patient. 'We're fishing for our bait right now. The big fish will come after the little fish we put on a trace.'

'You tie it then.' Fed up, Tony flung the rod on the rocks and walked sullenly to the back of the platform where he began tossing small stones at the water.

For a short while, the only sound apart from distant thunder was the waves lapping the rocks. Jeremy was the first to hook a yellowtail. It thrashed wildly as the hook bit deep into its mouth. As he reeled it in he almost forgot the storm. Tony came over to look at his brother's catch.

'Disgusting.' He poked the fish with his foot.

'Hey!' Ron's voice was sharp. 'We're putting this out live. Keep your feet off it, mate.' Tony scuffed the edge of the shallow rockpool where the silvery creature lay, its gills heaving.

'Cruel, if you ask me.'

'Nobody asked you.' The fisherman ignored him and began threading a large hook through the back of the fish. He handed the line to Jeremy.

'Cast out as far as you can.'

As Jeremy let the line fly out from the spool, the fish tumbled in a silver arc against the black water. A huge clap of thunder reverberated around the rocks, and at the same instant the entire scene became daylight and just as suddenly fell back into inky blackness. With a cry like an injured animal, Jeremy flung himself face down on the rocks, his hands over his head, trying to ward off the electric storm overhead. As the lightning took hold again he began to sob, loudly and uncontrollably. The other boys looked away in embarrassment. Tony put his arm around his brother.

'Don't cry, Jezza,' he crooned softly, 'the storm'll be gone soon. Don't cry.'

Ron picked up the rod that Jeremy had let go and stuck it deep into a crack. The reel hummed as the little yellow-tail swam for its life in the dark water.

'Don't like storms myself,' he said to no one in particular. 'Always like to pick a spot with a deep overhang when I'm fishing. Just in case a storm blows up.' Ron gestured towards the cliff behind them. 'There's a cave back there. You might be more comfortable in there till this front passes.'

Tony looked gratefully at him.

'Jeremy had a bad fright in a storm when he was a little kid.'

'Stays with you, that kind of thing.' Ron looked over at the other two boys. 'I've got my hands full right now. It would help if you kept your eye on your brother's rod. If it dips suddenly, give a shout.' He left them sitting together as the rain began to fall heavily. Thunder cannoned off the headland across the bay. Jeremy's breathing was ragged. He shivered uncontrollably.

'Sorry, Tony,' he managed.

'No worries.'

A few metres away the rod dipped wildly.

Somewhere deep below the surface a huge fish struggled against an invisible hunter. The reel began to scream as the line ran off at an incredible speed. The fish dived. The rod bounced out of the crack and slammed against the rock.

'Jeremy, do something! The rod'll be in the harbour in a second!'

Jeremy hesitated. With a wild shout Tony sprang. He felt the weight of the fish at once. The rod was like a living thing; it bucked and thrashed in his unsteady hands. He tried to reel in but the fish dived again, taking more line with it. Ron appeared at his elbow.

'Slowly, slowly. Let him feel he's winning. When he slows down, reel in quickly. Keep the tip of the rod up while you do it.' The instructions came thick and fast. From the safety of the cave Jeremy called, 'Don't lose him, Tony.'

The other boys had let go their own rods and stood

cheering him on. Tony had to plant his entire body behind the rod, bent almost in half.

'Jezza!' He shouted. 'Help me!'

The jewfish was hard to carry home. It weighed at least ten kilos. Their father couldn't stop slapping them on the back and laughing. Their mother smiled.

Somewhere, far away, the storm blew itself out.

THE PERFECT LUNCH

Lenora Luffhead had hair the colour of straw, and she was the only vegetarian in fifth grade.

At lunch she sat at the far end of the sheltershed so no one could see what she was eating. Her food disappeared down her throat in small silent gulps. If it was hard food, her jaws would pound up and down like pistons; whole carrots were pulverised in seconds by her sharp little teeth. Lettuce and parsley and soft white beans Lenora swallowed secretly; they made her limp inside. Everyone knew they could frighten Lenora Luffhead as easy as winking.

Danny McGee was a meat eater and proud of it. He was tall and strong, and his body had a thick layer of fat over it that kept him warm and powerful. His lunch, if his

mother made it, was cold sausages sandwiched between
slices of soft white bread spread thickly with butter. She
always put in an apple, the skin peeled round and round
and wound back onto the fruit, or a stick of celery. His
mother believed in salad. If his father made his lunch then
it was thick, uneven chunks of bread, chopped through
while it was still frozen, with liverwurst and butter in
deep slices as though they were spread with a chisel. There
was no fruit.

The best fun was to make Lenora cry. She was so pale
and thin, she had none of the fat of her carnivorous class-
mates. She swept across the yard like a little straw broom,
trying to keep herself stiff and ready for attack. Playtime
or class time made no difference to Lenora. She had no
friends and there was nothing she could do that was better
or different from anything anyone else could do. The
opportunities for taunting her were endless. She was a
small grey magnet for bullies. In an instant she might be
surrounded by jeering, laughing faces that did not leave
until she cried. The moment her tiny eyes filled up with
tears the crowd would begin to disperse. By the time her
face was awash with salty water she was alone. It was not
the crying anyone wanted to watch, it was just the fact
that they could make her do it that was funny.

Danny McGee was in training to be a bully. He watched the bigger boys closely. He saw how they pinched and shoved in line until some kid got into trouble for turning around and shouting at them. How they lied like sweet-faced angels to the teachers. How they teased and tormented the small and defenceless kids, like Lenora Luffhead.

It was Danny who worked out the masterly device of waiting until a boy was close to Lenora, then calling out in a sing-song voice, 'You love Lenora, you love Lenora,' till the boy exploded with anger.

'I do not, I do not.'

'You want to kiss her!'

'Notnotnotnotnot!'

'You love Lenora, you love Lenora.' The cry was taken up by those closest, and in moments a great gang of kids were chanting and laughing and Lenora's eyes were filling with tears. Danny had observed that the art of successful bullying lay in leaving your target at the right moment, just before the teacher on duty turned up, or in Lenora's case, as soon as she cried. He had no idea what Lenora did after he wandered off, and he didn't care.

What she did was stay exactly where she was for at least three minutes; she had learned that if she ran away too suddenly the bullies would scent new sport, and come after her like a pack of terriers nipping at her ankles. For the same reason she never wiped her eyes, and she tried not to cry loudly. When she was sure that she was alone and unobserved, she crept quietly into the nearest corner and faced the wall or the fence or just stared at the ground. Lenora wanted to be invisible to even an ant or a fly. She never said anything to her mother or father about the bullies. She didn't want to see their faces turn sad and their pale eyes fill with tears for her.

Danny McGee grew more powerful, and since Lenora was the perfect target, he soon spent most of his time trying his tactics out on her first.

Lenora suffered in silence, until one day she had an idea. It was so surprising an idea that she wondered how she could possibly have thought of it. It could not have come from her meek and timid mind, it must have some-how crept in from the minds of her tormentors because it was the kind of idea that any bully would have been proud of.

Before lunch one Wednesday she asked to be excused from the room, and as soon as the door closed behind her she made straight for her school bag. She took her lunch, chickpeas in a brown sauce with chopped carrot and parsley, and looked around for Danny McGee's bag. She checked the hall nervously to see if anyone else was coming, then like lightning she took out his lunch box and swapped her lunch for his. She slipped back into the room without anyone noticing her at all.

At lunch she made sure she sat as close as possible to Danny McGee; she wanted to watch his face when he opened his box.

It was better than she could ever have imagined. He lifted the lid and went quite pale. His eyes bulged and he made small gagging noises. It did not occur to him for an instant that this was not his lunch. His mother had started to make this kind of stuff for dinner; she was getting weirder and weirder about food. He was immensely hungry, but he could not possibly eat that mess. He cast around for someone else's lunch, intending to tip his own into a bin and snatch some other kid's food. But before he could, Lenora's small thin voice said loudly, 'Danny McGee's eating dog's vomit.'

The effect was instantaneous. Everyone looked into his lunch box and kids reeled backwards, retching and gagging, laughing and shouting, 'McGee's got vomit for lunch!'

He tried to shut the lid but someone grabbed the box out of his hands.

'Have a look at McGee's lunch, willya. He musta puked before he came to school this morning and put it in his lunch box.'

The food slopped over the edge, and in seconds it was all over Danny McGee. He was covered in brown slimy juice with chickpeas and bits of carrot and parsley stuck to his hair and face. Kids held their sides laughing, swaying unsteadily against one another in an ocean of sound.

Danny McGee sat stock still for a moment then leapt to his feet and made a dash for the taps. The crowd followed like one animal, hot on the scent of even greater fun.

Lenora Luffhead stayed where she was. She didn't laugh until the shed was completely empty. Then she laughed and laughed as another, even worse idea popped into her head.

When the class lined up for assembly after lunch, she stood directly behind Danny. He didn't notice her, which was a pity for him, although he could never have guessed what she planned to do. She waited until the whole school had fallen silent and the headmaster had stepped up to the microphone. Then she leaned forward and tapped

Danny on the shoulder, a light little tap, hardly likely to alert him to danger. He turned his face fully towards her, his damp hair sticking to his head in a most unattractive way. His eyes squinted into the sun and he was momentarily blinded. At that instant Lenora Luffhead leaned forward and kissed him wetly straight on the mouth, her lips making squashy noises as they ground into his face.

'Girls germs, no returns,' she whispered sweetly, leaning back.

The kids nearest her gasped with the shock of it, then clapped their hands over their mouths and choked back their laughter, desperately trying not to draw attention to themselves as the headmaster droned on out the front. The whole school knew about it before he had even finished speaking.

Danny McGee never mentioned his lunch, or the kiss, to his mother. He just asked if he could make lunch for himself, which was a mistake because his mother decided he had grown up and never made his lunch again. He ate peanut butter sandwiches for the rest of the year because he never got up in time to make anything more interesting.

He had to give up being a bully. It was too hard when even the littlest kids called him Chickpea McGee.

As Old As Mr Porter

No one believes Mr Porter poured water through the chimney at our house. I was there and I saw it. The fire was going, and my mum couldn't work out why there was suddenly water pouring out over the carpet. Now we're getting new carpet, which Mum has been wanting for ages. She thinks Mr Porter did us a favour. Dad reckons he's a lunatic.

'The man's mad, Doreen. He should be locked up, not let loose with all the CFS equipment.'

The CFS is short for the Country Fire Service. My dad and Mr Porter are both volunteer firefighters.

'He's usually harmless, Ted.' My mum speaks really softly, even when she's angry, which is hardly ever.

'How can you possibly say he's harmless? Look what

he did to our house!' Dad shouts at the top of his lungs when his blood pressure is up.

I knew why Mr Porter put the fire hose down our chimney. Because there was smoke pouring out of it and he thought we were all away. Dad reckons that's the stupidest thing he's ever heard. He says Mr Porter should have at least knocked on the door to see if anyone was home before he cranked out the hose and stuck it down the hole in the roof.

'He turned a whacking great fire hose on, climbed a twenty-foot ladder and pointed it down our chimney! He flooded the lounge room, for crying out loud. There is no excuse for doing something like that without at least knocking on the door.'

'He was just trying to help.' Mum was cooking tea. The only way you could tell she was getting annoyed was the way she kept tapping the wooden spoon against the side of the saucepan.

'Every time that idiot tries to help he ends up destroying other people's property. It's a good thing they're going to bring in compulsory retirement from the CFS. He's too old, that's half his problem.' Dad gave Mum a squeeze around the waist. 'Now don't go sticking up for him, you're always looking out for a hopeless case to help.'

Mum sighed. 'You'll be old one day, maybe then you'll realise what it's like to be made to retire from something you love.' She had that look on her face like Dad had better not try to say something funny this time. He didn't. He's pretty smart when it comes to Mum. She just has to give him a hug and he agrees with anything she says. Craig Levensworth came round here one day and while he was here Mum and Dad hugged each other three times. Craig reckons he's never seen his mum and dad hug— ever. I think he was pretty impressed, really.

I thought about Mr Porter at school that day, and I wondered what it was like to live alone and be old like he was. At lunchtime I asked Craig if he'd ever thought about getting old.

'Not if I can help it,' he said.

'What do you think it's going to be like?'

'I dunno, just so long as I don't end up like my great-granny. She's ninety-four and she dribbles.'

I'd seen Craig's great-granny. She had long hairs growing out of her chin. They were gross.

'She hardly eats anything either. Just a tiny bit of custard or stewed apple. She'd probably like baby food if you gave it to her.' Craig shuddered. 'I don't want to get so old I have to eat baby food. And she lives in a home. I don't want to have to go and live in one of those places.'

I remembered the time I went with Craig to visit his great-granny at the nursing home. She was sitting up in bed in this little room with hardly any furniture. There was one photo on the chest of drawers, but nothing else anywhere. It was depressing.

'What about if you lived by yourself at home though, that'd be better. You could have parties and stay up late— anything you want.' I tried to imagine Mr Porter having a party. It didn't seem likely.

'The trouble is, you're too old to do that stuff. You'd just have to sit around and watch the cobwebs growing.' Craig was definitely getting worked up about the idea of getting old. I changed the subject.

I was still thinking about it when I got home that afternoon. Mum had a huge cake on the bench, iced and everything.

'It's not for you, Eric,' she flicked my hand away from the icing. 'It's for Mr Porter. It's his birthday today. He's seventy. I'm taking it down there in a minute, do you want to come?'

I had a brilliant idea.

'Mum, what about instead of us taking the cake down there, we have a bit of a party for him here?'

Mum gave me a hug. 'That's a nice idea. You get on your bike and ride around and ask people. I'll make some scones while you're gone. Tell everyone: five o'clock, here. We'll have a light supper.'

I asked every old person in the street. They all said they'd come, even though I wasn't too sure some of them even knew Mr Porter. At five o'clock all these people started to stream through our front door. Mum was a bit taken aback. She sent me down the street to get biscuits and ham from the deli. When I got home the place was hopping. Everywhere there were oldies having loud conversations with each other. I never saw that much white hair and wrinkles in one room before. Mr Porter was grinning away in the corner, surrounded by a bunch of old ladies who didn't seem to mind the fact that half his teeth weren't there.

When Dad got home there were five couples dancing on the new carpet in the lounge room and a group playing cards at the kitchen table. Dad didn't even ask what was happening. He just got a beer out of the fridge and joined the men on the back verandah. He was pretty nice to Mr Porter; I watched him for a while. He told a few jokes and laughed at the ones the old blokes told.

After everyone went home Mum and Dad both collapsed onto the couch. The oldies had washed everything up and put it all away and the place was cleaner than before the party. Mum hugged Dad. Dad smiled. 'I had a really good chat to old Porter. Did you know he started this local CFS branch when he was forty? Same age as I am now.'

I looked at Dad really hard. He was forty, I was ten and Mr Porter was seventy.

In thirty years time, I would be as old as Dad was now, Dad would be as old as Mr Porter, and Mr Porter, well, he would probably be dead.

When I went to bed that night I thought about it all again. Thirty years is a really long time. Sixty years is forever. I tried to imagine how long it would take, but I couldn't. I tried to imagine what I would look like, but I couldn't. In the end I stopped thinking about it, it was too hard. I couldn't imagine ever being as old as Mr Porter.

MAGGOT AND MR LITTLE

There are rules for fat boys. Maggot McGuire told them to me, even though I'm not fat.

Maggot is huge.

'Always wear your shirt outside your trousers, that's one rule,' he said.

I could see the sense of that. 'So your stomach doesn't look like pudding spilling out of a bowl; is that why, Maggot?'

'Of course,' he said, 'that one's easy.'

'What's another rule?' I asked. We were flopped on the ground behind the lunch shed. I checked to see if my stomach looked like runaway pudding; it didn't.

'Make sure your fly is done up. Fat boys often have their fly undone.'

'It's the runaway pudding, isn't it? It pushes their fly down.' My fly was zipped up tight. I looked.

'Mmm.' Maggot made circles in the dust with his big white hands. 'Avoid mirrors and going shopping.' He began to pile small stones in the circles.

'I don't like shopping much. My mum still wants to come into the change rooms with me.' I pulled a face to show Maggot how much I hated that.

'A fat boy's mum can't fit in the change room,' he said.

I hadn't thought of that. We were silent for a minute. I threw some gravel at the fence; it pinged off the tin like gunfire.

'Want to play war?' I asked. 'We could pretend these are grenades.' I pointed to the stones he had heaped up alongside him. 'Chuck them at the fence.'

'Nah. That's another rule, no exercise unless you're made to.' He grinned.

A kindy kid poked his head around the shed and stared at us. Maggot growled and swiped his huge arm in the air like a claw. The kid disappeared like a shot.

'Fat boys have to be tough,' he said. 'A nice fat boy is dead meat.'

Maggot heaved himself up off the ground and steadied

himself against the shed wall. I jumped up too. The lunch bell was about to go.

'Wanna have some Weetbix at my house after school?' I asked. 'I can fit eight in a bowl, easy.'

'Unreal!'

I knew he was impressed.

We walked back across the playground. Kids scattered ahead of us. Maggot was like a bull elephant; slow but powerful. No one wanted to tangle with him. I tried to imagine what it felt like to be so big. You could hear his thighs rubbing together through his trousers, and his arms swishing noisily against his shirt. He pulled a big handkerchief from his pocket and wiped his face and hands.

'Carry a couple of handkerchiefs is another rule,' he wheezed a little bit as he walked. 'Fat boys sweat a lot.'

I nodded my head; I could see that was true.

'Why don't you take off your jumper?' I asked. He had a woollen jumper tied around his waist like a thick belt.

'Tool of the trade.' He winked at me. 'Wait till we go in. I'll show you what I mean.'

The classroom was hot and airless. Maggot slid his jumper off and rolled it into a tight, thick wad. He put it carefully on his seat and sat down on it. 'Watch this,' he whispered across the aisle. His great body seemed to shudder, his eyes closed and a smile spread slowly across his face. I wondered what he was doing. It was Mr Little who asked the question out loud.

'McGuire!' he roared, 'What are you doing there, boy?'

'Nothing, Sir.' Maggot looked innocent.

Mr Little crashed down the aisle towards him. 'Rubbish!' he roared and leant right over Maggot's huge body. 'Stand up, boy!'

'I don't think that's a good idea, Sir,' Maggot said. I held my breath. Mr Little shook with fury.

'Stand up!' he shouted.

Maggot stood up. The kids nearest him went pale and gagged. Mr Little got most of it in a great lungful of foul air. He went green and ran for the door.

Maggot shrugged his shoulders at me. 'It's best if you let the fart stay in your jumper,' he said. 'Fat boys are powerful farters.'

TREASURE

Jordan blinked. Maybe it was a trick of the light; it was pretty dark behind the bus shelter.

No, it was still there. He looked around cautiously. Had anyone else seen it? He thought not. It was big; maybe it wouldn't fit in his bag. For a moment he considered unloading his books and leaving them behind on the ground. Better not. He was already two days late with his science project. Another excuse for not doing it, and he'd get a detention for sure.

Under his school blazer maybe. It might fit. He imagined trying to sit down on the bus with his coat bulging. No good. Frazier Elliot would rip his coat open for sure; that kid was such a jerk.

He decided to throw his raincoat over it and carry it

underneath; just as well he still had his raincoat in his bag, it hadn't rained for months but it paid to be ready. Swiftly he pulled the crumpled raincoat out and threw it over his find. His fingers tingled, as though a small electric current had passed through them. He could hear the bus coming so he grabbed his treasure and his bag and stood at the end of the line. All the little kids were pushing and shoving, trying to weasel past the big kids. Usually he would have been in there with the best of them, elbows flying, today he was content to stand at the back of the line.

It was Friday, everyone was hanging out to get home for the long weekend. The bus squealed to a stop about five metres past the queue of screaming kids. The line broke into a seething mass of pushing and shoving.

The bus driver swivelled in his seat and roared, 'Get down the back, you kids.' A tiny space appeared near the front. Satisfied he had made room for more, the bus driver lifted himself up in his seat and shouted down at the doorway, 'Only five more, the rest of you'll have to wait for the 303.'

A groan went up from the kids who were not going to get on. Jordan saw his chance and threw himself at the step just as the driver closed the door. He wasn't going to wait another half hour tonight. He wanted to get home and examine his treasure in the privacy of his room.

'I should put you off, you little mongrel,' the driver grumbled. 'I said no more.' He took his frustration out on the rest of the passengers. 'You kids shut up or I'll put you off.'

Jordan clutched the raincoat so tight, the tips of his fingers felt like they had pins and needles. As the bus drew away, something caught his eye and he tried to see through the dirty glass door. It could have been someone behind the bus shelter; it looked like someone stooping down, looking for something.

Trevor Blainey got off at his stop with him. Jordan could have done without Trevor Blainey tonight. He walked ahead as fast as he could, pretending he hadn't seen him.

'Oiy, Jordan, wait up, what's the rush?' Blainey was a pain sometimes. 'You doing anything over the weekend? Wanna come over?'

Jordan sighed, there was no way he was going to be able to shake him; he couldn't walk fast enough with his bag and his raincoat-covered loot.

'What have you got in mind?'

'I dunno, kick the footy maybe?' Trevor was anxious to please. 'My dad's got a new boat. It's a four-metre tinny. He might let us take it out.'

'Sure, and pigs might fly, too.' Jordan hitched up his raincoat. It was dragging on the ground and he was afraid he would trip.

'Why are you carrying your raincoat? It hasn't rained for weeks.' Trevor tugged at the yellow plastic. 'Did you find it in lost property? I left mine there for two terms once. Mum reckoned she was going to make me buy the next one out of my pocket money if I didn't find it.'

'Yeah, I got it out of lost property. Now flick off, I'm busy.'

Jordan turned in at his gate. Trevor stared after him, mystified.

'What's up your nose anyway?' He scuffed his shoe on the concrete and tucked his hands in his pockets. Jordan heard him muttering as he walked away.

Jordan's mother and father were already home. That was unusual; they both worked and usually they didn't get home till six.

'Just dump that old load of school junk right here, my lovely,' his mother said, smiling. 'We are going away for the weekend!' His father was beaming. They must have won the lottery or something!

'Where to?' Jordan hung on to his raincoat and school bag.

'To the south coast. I can't wait! Your father's boss is lending him the company beach house for the weekend, fully stocked with food and towels and blankets. I've already packed your clothes, kiddo, so let's just hop in the car and go. If we don't leave right now we'll get stuck in traffic and won't be there for hours.' His mother swept his things out of his arms and gave him a little push in the back. 'Let's go, let's go. Time's a-wasting.'

'I have to bring my things, Mum.' Jordan searched wildly for a reason to collect the raincoat. 'I've got to finish my science project.'

'Well if that's your idea of a weekend away, it's not mine.' His mother grabbed his school bag and shoved him through the door. 'I bet you don't write a single word.' She laughed. 'South coast, here we come.' Jordan was in the car and on the road before he could complain.

'I've left my raincoat behind, we have to go back and get it.' It was a feeble attempt and he knew it. His mother and father laughed uproariously. 'One whole weekend of perfect weather coming up.' His father tapped the wheel and hummed. 'No one needs a raincoat where we're going.'

Jordan sank down in the seat. He felt like crying. Under the raincoat in the hallway was an unexplored treasure and now he was going to have to wait all weekend before he could look at it properly.

The beach shack was like a palace. There were ocean views from every window. The kitchen was all white and shiny and new. None of the glasses were chipped, the crockery all matched and the place even had a dishwasher.

'See,' his dad said, 'It won't be too bad, you'll only have to stack the dishwasher and empty it.'

His mother cracked up laughing. Jordan didn't get the joke. His fingers were hurting, his hands felt weird, like the skin was too tight on them. He rubbed them together and a hot rush of blood surged up his arms. He was almost knocked over by it.

'Steady on, only joking. You don't really have to stack the dishwasher.' His dad peered at him. 'Are you okay? You've gone a funny colour.'

'Car sick.' Jordan put his hand over his mouth and ran into the bathroom. He made gagging noises and flushed the toilet, hoping his mother and father wouldn't come in. Something strange was happening to his whole body. He felt light and hot. The skin on his hands was thrumming like a musical instrument. He cradled his head in his hands. Instantly his head cleared and he felt better. He went back out.

'That must have done some good. You're the right colour again.' His father ruffled his hair and it stood completely on end. 'Wow, you've got a real static charge in you tonight. Better sit down before you fuse the place.'

Jordan collapsed into the nearest chair. He had no idea what was going on, or what would happen next.

'Are you hungry, sweetheart?' His mother bent over him.

'No thanks.' He shook his head. Food was out of the question.

'Well then, what about you hit the sack, kiddo. You look bushed. You can get up early tomorrow morning and go for a walk on the beach. Take the first room down the corridor, and don't worry about brushing your teeth.'

His father laughed. 'That'll be the day.'

Jordan slipped under the blankets, without getting undressed, and pulled them up to his chin. He didn't feel frightened, but he did feel apprehensive. Something strange but wonderful was happening to him.

He dreamed he was at the bus stop. He was looking through the bus door again. Behind the shelter was a bag lady, all bent and wrinkled and dirty, poking about in the rubbish. She was muttering under her breath, pulling a shopping trolley full of bags, rubbish and junk, and bits of old food. He tried to open the door but he couldn't. Frazier was in front of him. Jordan found himself wrestling the other boy as the bus drove away.

He woke up feeling as though an electric charge had just pumped through his body. It was already light outside, so he pulled on his shoes and opened the front door. He had to get out onto the beach. Had to watch the sunrise. Somewhere on the way down to the sand he took off his shoes and left them behind, feeling the cool grains sifting between his toes like hard water. A feeling of joy he didn't remember ever feeling before filled him up. The sun rose the way the happiness rose in him. Jordan ran along the edge of the water kicking and splashing and shouting.

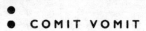

There was no one in sight, and no other house for miles.
He felt free.

Where the sandhills came down to the shore he turned inland. A rocky inlet fed out to the sea. Ants were running all over the rocks. He squatted down to get a closer look. A large lump of driftwood lay in the sand at his feet. Idly he picked it up and started to squash the ants, enjoying the crunch as they crumpled under his stick, until his hands began to feel cold and he had to put the driftwood down and rub them. This was so odd. The ants lay in small piles where he had killed them, and he felt inexplicably sad. His hands were getting colder and colder. He laid his palms over the dead ants and instantly felt the heat return to his hands. Underneath the palms began to tickle, something wriggled and struggled to get away. The ants were alive! He flicked his hands backwards in fear and ants ran in all directions. This could not be happening.

He ran back to the beach house without stopping to pick up his shoes, flung open the door and threw himself inside. His heart rattled like a mad thing in his chest and he couldn't get a breath.

'Good grief, Jordan, what's the matter?' His mother

was staring at him from the hallway. 'You're making enough noise to wake the dead.'

Wake the dead. Jordan fainted clean away.

His mother made him spend the rest of the day in bed. She got a pile of comics from somewhere and brought him chocolate and lemonade. He lay there uncomplaining. It didn't feel safe to go outside just yet.

He dreamed of the bus again. Frazier Elliot was punching him. Sinking the boot in and calling him names. Jordan hit him with a huge lump of driftwood that materialised in his hand and Frazier fell down dead. Jordan's hands were like ice; he rubbed them and rubbed them but nothing happened. He knew he had to put them on Frazier, but he couldn't.

This time, when he woke up he felt frightened. He crept down the hall to his parents' room and climbed into their bed. He hadn't been in bed with his mum and dad for ages. His mother cuddled him sleepily.

'What's up, kiddo?' She nuzzled his head with her chin.

'I don't feel good.'

'You must be coming down with something. It'll probably turn into a fever and a sore throat. Stay inside this morning and take it easy.' She drifted back to sleep.

The morning dragged on and on. Hot chocolate and croissants did not make him feel any better.

'I need some fresh air.' He walked to the door. 'I think I'll go for a walk on the beach.'

'Put a jumper on.'

He sighed. His mother was so protective.

'You should stay put.' She looked worried.

'I'm fine, Mum. I feel better. Honestly. I just need some exercise.'

He was out the door before she could argue.

As soon as he had left the house he felt better; he felt light and happy again. He ran and jumped on the sand, kicking dust storms ahead of him and dodging the drift. He could feel the tingling in his hands but now it felt nice and warm. He thought of the treasure in his front hall at home. The way his fingers had tingled when he first touched it. The pins and needles feeling in his hands on the bus. His body buzzed.

On the sand in front of him lay a dead and desiccated fish, no longer even smelly. Jordan picked it up and laid it in the palm of his left hand. He passed his right hand over the top of it and closed his eyes. The fish began to feel slimy, then slippery. He opened his eyes in wonder as it suddenly flipped out of his grasp and thrashed about on the sand. It was alive! He nudged it into the ocean with his foot and watched it swim away. He could bring the dead to life!

'I'll be famous.' The thought astonished and then scared him. He realised with a thump that he did not want to be famous like that: the press hounding him, every sick person in the world knocking on his door. 'I'll hide it.' That was a more comforting thought. He could just use it when he needed to; if his family got sick or if a friend was hurt.

The sea was turning grey and angry, the sky had become dark. It looked as if a storm was coming up fast from the south. By the time he reached the house heavy pellets of rain were slapping into his skin and bouncing off the sand. He was wet and cold, and the tingle in his hands was no longer warming.

'Dad and I have decided to go back a bit early, kiddo.' His mother tried to make it sound cheerful. 'Living in the lap of luxury is a bit boring. We thought we'd better check on the cockroaches at home. Make sure they haven't missed us.'

He knew that he'd been acting strange and both parents were worried. He began to feel nervous. At home was his treasure, still hidden under the raincoat in the hall. The very thought made his hands tingle again.

The drive home was slow. 'Looks like half the people who went away for the weekend have decided to leave early,' his dad muttered.

'Maybe they've all got cockroaches to get home to as well,' laughed his mum. Jordan stared out of the window lost in thought. By the time they pulled into the driveway he knew what he had to do.

He rode his bike as fast as he could, balancing the thing on the handlebars. When he reached the bus shelter he jumped off and, without looking at it once, he slid it onto the ground in the exact same position he had found it. He rode home without a backward glance.

That night he dreamed again; of the bag lady, poking around on the ground at the back of the bus shelter. He saw her eyes light up as she spotted his treasure. Saw the look of greed and fear as she picked it up, saw her fingers twitch and the way her face changed. She put it on her shopping trolley and covered it up with a piece of brown paper. Jordan watched her shuffle away, looking for a place to examine her find in peace.

Frazier Elliot eyed him with great suspicion.

'What are you asking me over for?' he asked Jordan. 'I thought you hated me.'

Jordan smiled. 'I've changed,' he said.

TEACHER TRAINING

Everybody had to help pitch the tents. There were eighty-five children plus five teachers, and between them there were only two people who knew anything about putting up a tent. It took ages before they were all up, and a lot of those tents were never going to make it through the first weak breeze.

Glenda and Phoebe and Britt and I were all sharing a tent. When Mr Ford checked on our group he clutched his forehead and pretended to fall backwards in horror. 'Who was responsible for putting you lot together? Were they sane?'

He was right. Someone should have figured out that

putting the four of us in a tent together for five days was going to be a disaster; we hated each other like poison.

Glenda likes to make the rules. Straight away she told everyone where they were going to sleep, and the most incredible argument broke out. Britt was frothing at the mouth. She and Glenda were shouting in each other's faces, so Phoebe and I went and picked our spots and put our bags down. That made both the others go completely crazy. In a matter of seconds World War III broke out. It only stopped because the centre pole collapsed and the tent fell down around us. It took forever to get it back up. Everyone else was standing in line for dinner and we were still burrowing around under metres of canvas.

We were the last to eat. It was a barbecue dinner, too. When we finally got our food it was cold. I just ate the salad and bread rolls. Glenda ate all hers and so did Britt. It was as if they were competing to see who could be the most gross. Phoebe picked all the lettuce out of the salad, which left her with a few soggy bits of tomato and some celery.

'You look so stupid, you know.' It really annoyed me

the way she sucked the tomato between her teeth so she left the skin behind.

'Just shut up, Elizabeth.' She had a cheekful of tomato skins and she was picking them out with her fingers and laying them down in little rows on the plate.

'Why don't you shut up as well, Phoebe?' Britt suggested sweetly. 'That would make a nice change.'

Glenda threw up her hands. 'We've got five days together in this tent! I can't stand it, I'm going to call Mum and tell her I'm sick. I'd rather be sick than be with you lot.'

'You're always sick, Glenda,' Britt snapped. 'And *I'm* getting sick now, too—sick of you!'

'How original.' Glenda has this way of saying things so they sound totally slimy. Britt ignored her.

'As far as I'm concerned we should agree on a few things now.' Britt's just like Glenda: bossy and full of herself.

'Who died and left you in charge?' Phoebe was still sucking tomatoes. 'I wouldn't agree with you if my life depended on it.'

I could see what was coming. I climbed into my sleeping bag without brushing my teeth.

For the next four days the tent was a battleground. We

had not spoken one nice word to each other, and we all refused to take any responsibility for keeping the place tidy. Every pair of socks I had brought with me was gone; I only had one jumper left and that was because I slept in it. When the sun streamed through the tent flap on the morning of the last day we were lying in a mound of clothes that covered the groundsheet.

Britt got up first and tried to roll me off the clothes that were half under my sleeping bag. Naturally I objected, but it's hard to fight back when you're zipped to the chin in a bag. I ended on my front, face down in someone else's socks. Glenda and Phoebe woke up and started arguing about who had the mosquito repellent. I felt around for it at the bottom of my sleeping bag and threw it at them.

'You don't need this stuff,' I shouted, 'you're both totally repellent to any living creature!' I dragged my towel out from under Phoebe's rucksack, shook the red dirt off it, flicked away something that looked like the first night's dinner and stomped off to the showers.

When I got back the other three were racing out through the tent flap, screaming and shouting at each other. It was chaos. Mr Ford got there at the same time I did.

'I wasn't here when it happened!' I wasn't going to be blamed for this. 'I don't even *know* what happened.'

Mr Ford peered inside the tent and then jumped back. I had a quick look. On my sleeping bag there was a short fat snake with a diamond-shaped tail.

'A death adder, if I'm not mistaken.' Mr Ford was taking it very calmly.

'What are we going to do?' Britt looked really worried.

'Shoot it,' Glenda said. She looked around for support. 'Well, what's wrong with that?' She got huffy straight away.

'For one thing, it's my sleeping bag, Glenda, and I don't want holes all over it, not to mention mashed snake.' I turned to Mr Ford.

'What should we do, Sir?'

He cupped his chin in his hand and thought. 'Actually, I don't know,' he said finally. 'But you know what? I haven't seen you girls do one thing together this camp. I'll give you an hour to think about it. If you manage to come up with a plan that's going to work, come and get me. I'll be having my breakfast over there.' He pointed to the far side of the camp. 'Make a communal decision, girls. Best of luck.' As he strolled off, I noticed his shoulders were shaking.

'Well, if you won't shoot it, then poison it.' Glenda was not exactly an environmentalist. 'Put some Ratsak in there.'

'This is a snake, not a rat, you idiot!' Phoebe was obviously thinking about this. 'I say we set fire to the tent. That way we kill two birds with one stone. We get rid of the snake and we don't have to pack.'

I almost laughed, except Phoebe was probably serious. It was just the sort of dumb thing she *would* do.

'Look.' Britt had her I'm-in-charge voice on. 'Obviously we're not going to burn the tent down, Phoebe. And we haven't got a gun or Ratsak for that matter, Glenda. Do you have an opinion about this, Elizabeth?'

'My opinion is the three of you should step inside with the snake for a while.' I smirked.

'Oh, terrific, Elizabeth.' Britt snorted through her nose at me like a horse. Immediately Phoebe started to paw the ground with her foot and Glenda whinnied. They both galloped around outside the tent, laughing like mad.

'Whenever you're ready,' Britt said in an icy voice, 'perhaps we can *discuss* this?'

Phoebe and Glenda collapsed on the ground together, giggling.

'Now I want a sensible suggestion from each of us, starting with you, Elizabeth.' Britt always sounds like she's twenty-five, instead of thirteen.

'I say we leave it there.'

'Well, why should *we* get the thing out? A teacher should do it, not us.' Glenda pouted.

'What if we get bitten?' Phoebe shuddered.

'If I get bitten, my father will sue the school for every penny they've got.' Glenda looked pleased at the idea.

'Exactly.' Britt leaned towards us and dropped her voice. 'Have any of you wondered why a teacher would leave four teenage girls alone with a death adder and tell them to work out what to do?'

We all thought about it for a second. The light dawned at the same moment for each of us.

'It's a fake snake,' we all said at once.

'He must have put it in there after you went to the shower,' Britt pointed her finger at me. 'He could have shoved it in under the side without us seeing.'

'He could have put a ticking bomb in the tent and none of you would have seen it,' I muttered.

'True.' Britt actually smiled. Phoebe started to laugh and Glenda looked confused.

'Why would he do that? It's a pretty scary joke, isn't it? What if one of us had a heart attack from the fright?'

'God, Glenda, you are such a hypochondriac. Always thinking about how sick you could be. As if any of us is likely to have a heart attack.'

'But she's got a good point, Phoebe.' You could just about hear Britt's brain clicking over, 'Why *did* he do it?'

'Well, that's obvious,' I shot back. 'To get us to cooperate. It's probably some dumb trick he learned when he was training to go on camps.'

'Who cares? Why don't we just get the snake and chuck it at him. See if he jumps.'

Phoebe pulled back the tent flap and peered carefully at the snake. She threw Glenda's shoe at it just to be sure. The snake bounced sideways off the sleeping bag and lay upside down on the clothes. Phoebe carried it out triumphantly. 'A rather good rubber death adder.'

Glenda touched it gingerly. 'It looks real,' she said.

That gave me an idea.

'Give me that carry bag you've been hiding your lollies and chips in, Glenda, and don't try to say you haven't been stuffing your face since we got here.'

Glenda glared at me. 'Why should I?' she demanded.

'Because we're going to play a little camp trick of our own on Mr Ford.'

Suddenly they were all interested. We got the bag and I took them down to the edge of the scrub. I turned over a log and a huge blue-tongue lizard hissed at us. 'I saw this yesterday. Don't move, I'll grab its head and you hold the bag open.' I threw the lizard into the bag in one quick motion. It wriggled and squirmed so much the bag looked alive.

'Now let's find Mr Ford.'

When Mr Ford saw the writhing, squirming bag, I thought he was going to pass out. Glenda started squealing. 'Sir, Sir, we caught it! Elizabeth got it in the bag. She picked it up, Sir!'

'It's trying to get out,' Phoebe screamed. 'Quick, Elizabeth, let go of it before it bites you!' I tossed the bag at Mr Ford. He caught it in both hands and felt the thrashing weight of the blue-tongue under his fingers. He dropped the bag and fell backwards off his chair at the same time. All of us were screaming and squealing and leaping around. Mr Ford didn't see me catch the bag and let the lizard out.

'It's gone, sir.' I said calmly. 'Over there.' I pointed towards the teachers' tents.

We watched the teachers for a bit while they ran around like mad things. Then we went back to our tent and fell about laughing.

'I'm sort of sorry it's the last day, really,' Britt smiled. 'Now I can think of a whole pile of things we could do.'

'Well, there's always school next week.' Phoebe rubbed her hands together. 'I can't wait.'

'Which one of you stole my chips?' Glenda started throwing things, looking for them. In thirty seconds the tent was a battleground.

We were the last to get on the bus.

SOMETHING TO LAUGH ABOUT

Moving away was awful. I had to leave half my things behind because the house we've got now is about half the size. The local Salvation Army shop was bulging at the seams with all the things my mum took there. My wetsuit for a start.

'We'll be living in the mountains, for heaven's sake, there's no beach for fifty kilometres. Get used to it!'

Mum sounds like a siren when she gets going. You might as well complain about everything all at once because she's going to crank up the sound anyway.

'What about my surfboard, and my fish tank and my billycart? There must be hills I could ride the billycart down.'

'The hills are too steep and too dangerous for the billy-cart, Elizabeth, and anyway it's about time you started to look like a girl for a change and do things that are a bit more ladylike.'

I do look like a girl. I have long blonde hair and I wear dresses sometimes. I just like to do stuff with my brother. He's always been the only person who really makes me laugh. It's totally off that he's gone to live with Dad in Queensland. I'm never going to forgive him.

'Ty has decided to stay with Dad.' Mum had told me as if she was giving me a shopping list.

'What!' I was hysterical.

'Calm down, he'll come back in the holidays.'

'And I'll go away in the holidays!' I started to cry. I hate it when I cry. I feel like I've cried a lot in the last few months, too. First Mum and Dad decided to split up, then Dad got transferred to Brisbane and Mum bought a house in the mountains, then Ty went and betrayed me without even talking to me about it. I don't understand him. How could he do that? He reckons that he gets on better with Dad, and anyway Mum can't afford to keep him because he's growing so much he needs new clothes every two weeks.

'Don't go, Ty, please, I'll have no one to talk to. You can't go.' I was practically begging him. I would have paid him to stay if I'd had any money.

'It'll be all right, Sis.' He knows I hate being called Sis. He just did that to put me off. I kicked him in the shin.

'Oww! Why'd you do that?'

He knew why, though, he never did a thing to get back at me. He just stood there like a big log.

'I'll write to you. I'll tell you everything I'm doing.'

He got down on his haunches and put his hand on my shoulder. I flicked it straight off.

'Don't worry, you'll find new friends. Come on, crack a laugh, kiddo.'

There was nothing laugh about.

Mum made me join the Young Players; it's this group of total losers that puts on plays in the local hall twice a year.

Miss Jonquil is about a hundred and she runs the place. The first night I went she was picking kids to be partners in an acting game. You had to pretend your partner was really a member of your family and you were having an argument. Method Acting she calls it. She put this kid called Colin, who is a complete dork, with a girl called

Catherine Parr and told Catherine to be the wife and Colin to be the husband. They had to have an argument about housework.

Catherine got stuck right into it. You could see that one day she'd be doing this for real. Colin looked like he'd been hit in the head by a flying mullet. He stood with his mouth open and said absolutely nothing.

'Re-*act*, Colin,' Miss Jonquil said. Colin's lip twitched. He rolled his eyeballs back in his head, so he looked like something off the planet Dweebon, and a sort of choking sound came out of his mouth.

'Very *good*, Colin,' Miss Jonquil purred. 'This is very *real*.'

I couldn't believe my ears. Good! This was pathetic. Colin was just about unconscious on the floor with anxiety, and she was telling him it was good? Catherine kept ranting and raving and her voice got louder and louder. Colin's eyeballs were hanging out of his head, his lips had got all wet. I couldn't watch. I went out to the kitchen and made myself a cup of Milo. Another girl was out there already with a drink in her hand. We sort of smiled at each other and drank our Milo in silence. I never know what to say to total strangers in situations like that. After a minute she washed her cup out and went back into the hall.

Colin had progressed to slapping his damp palms on the table. You could hear this awful squishing sound as his skin flopped on the Laminex. Catherine was in full swing.

'And another thing, what about the toilet?'

Silence from Colin.

'Well, I've cleaned the toilet for the last time. It's going to just stink from now on as far as I'm concerned.'

I couldn't help it. I burst out laughing and Miss Jonquil gave me this freezing look. If looks could kill, I'd have been hanging from a hook. The girl who was out in the kitchen with me started to giggle and all of a sudden everyone was laughing. Colin actually looked pleased. I think he thought he'd done something clever. Catherine had her hands on her hips and was screaming, 'What's so funny? What's so funny?'

Miss Jonquil tried to calm everyone down, but in the end she couldn't and so she told this other girl and me to go outside because we kept starting each other off again, and then pretty soon everyone was giggling.

It was freezing outside. Mid-winter in the mountains is pretty cold. She told me her name and I told her mine and we went and crouched down under the rainwater tank at the side of the building.

'Do you want a cigarette?' She handed me a full packet of Benson and Hedges. I took one and played with it in my fingers for a while.

'I've got a lighter, if you want to smoke the thing.' She didn't seem to care if I did or not.

'No thanks. I tried one once before and it tasted foul.' I had just about died coughing, too.

'You get used to it.'

She lit up a fag and inhaled the smoke deep into her lungs. It came back out through her nostrils in little thin streams. Just the smell of it made me want to gag. I started to crumble the cigarette in my fingers, shredding the paper first into little ragged pieces, and shaking the tobacco over the ground.

'If you don't want to smoke it you could just give it back.' She didn't get angry but I could see she was annoyed.

'One less for you to kill yourself with,' I said. I looked her straight in the face. There was a grey film of smoke over her skin and she smelled pretty awful. 'You stink when you smoke, you know.'

'I know,' she said.

'Well, why do you do it?' I couldn't work her out. She was different from anyone else I had ever met.

'Just to make my mum mad.' Monica blew smoke rings in the air. 'Mum left Dad last year and she gave up smoking at the same time. It's been hell ever since. I figure I need some entertainment.'

'Have you got any brothers or sisters?' I was interested. We had at least one thing in common.

'A sister. She's older. She went to live with Dad.'

'Wow, you're kidding me. My mum and dad split up and my brother went to live with my dad.'

'Yeah?'

'Yeah. Dad's in Brisbane, though. I'm going to see him these holidays. My brother's coming down here to be with Mum. We're going to have a week together first, then I fly to Queensland.'

'Unreal. My dad's in Queensland too. I'm swapping with my sister in the holidays.'

We both just looked at each other. It was so weird. We started to laugh. Miss Jonquil came outside to call us back in and there we were, cracking up laughing.

Back inside, Catherine Parr and Colin were off in a corner staring soulfully at each other. Monica looked at me and I looked at her.

'It looks too real for them to be acting,' she whispered.
I burst out laughing.

Miss Jonquil sent us outside again.

Mum's pretty pleased that I like the Young Players so
much. I reckon she's a genius for thinking of it. The only
problem is I spend so much time outside, I have to wear
a beanie, gloves, two jumpers and a coat every time I go.

Monica and I are looking forward to Queensland.

WAR GAMES

Billy crashed through the door, banging his boots loudly on the wooden boards.

'Good morning, Dad.'

'Morning, son.'

'War games at Trenton today.'

'Oh?' His father collected a briefcase from under the table and adjusted his tie. 'Who's playing today?'

'Dad, it's called "engaging the enemy". We don't *play* war; that's for little kids. We have real war games. You have to be dead if you're hit. If you get hit three times, you're out.' He filled his bowl with Honey Smacks and poured sugar thickly over the top. 'Any chocolate milk?'

'I used it all last night. Ask Mrs Webly to buy more today, will you?'

Billy spooned Honey Smacks into his mouth. They didn't taste as good with plain milk. He made a mental note to tell the housekeeper to stockpile the stuff and freeze it.

'The key to the gun cupboard is on the dresser. Put it back when you've finished with it.'

The door closed behind him.

Billy had wanted to have his war games at Trenton for a long time, but Mrs Lender, who lived there, wouldn't let her precious Jeffrey play with guns.

'That man has lost all commonsense since his wife died. He has an arsenal of replica weapons, and he lets the child play with them. It's obscene.'

Jeffrey thought it would be wonderful to live like Billy. No stupid rules; it'd be heaps of fun. He didn't dare disobey *his* mother. But today she would be away until late, and Jeffrey had a babysitter who didn't care what he did as long as she could chat on the phone. This was a big day.

Billy whistled up the dog. 'Here boy, we're off to war.'

The terrier rushed out at him.

The other boys were already at Trenton when Billy got there with his heavy bag of guns. They had all lied to their mothers about what they were doing at Jeffrey's house today. They were shivering with the wonderful thought of holding those heavy weapons and ducking and weaving through the rocks and trees. Billy unloaded the bag onto the ground.

'The sten gun's for me. Jeffrey, you can have the Luger.' He felt generous for a moment. 'The rest of you can pick what you want.'

There was a mad scramble as the boys dived on the guns.

Billy stood up. 'I'm leading the good guys, see? David, you're with me. Sam, you're too slow to be useful. You're with me too, Allen. I guess that leaves you with Landon, Jeffy. Never mind. He's so thin he could hide behind a sapling and never be seen.'

Landon, who was tall and excruciatingly thin, blushed.

'Hang on, it's my garden you know, I should get to decide.' Jeffrey sounded pathetic, and the others looked away. Billy began to gather up the guns out of the boys' hands.

'Okay, if you feel that way I'll just go home.'

The Luger was too good to lose; Jeffrey gave in.

Billy was in charge.

'Now these are the rules. If you take a direct hit, you're dead, so fall down. You're out for five minutes. If you get hit twice then you're out for ten minutes. Three hits and you're out for good. First team to be all out loses. You have to keep the rules or you'll be executed.'

'Not really executed, right?' Sam looked nervous; this game was sounding pretty fierce.

Billy ignored him. 'Right, I've got a box of blanks. We'll load them up now. Just sit the red cap over the brass shells and fit them into your guns. When they go off they'll sound just like real.'

The boys pulled their magazines out and began stuffing them with the blanks. They were excited and laughing— this was going to be great. Jeffrey struggled to unclip his magazine. It was jammed; he couldn't budge it.

'This thing won't move, Billy,' he complained. 'The trigger's all jammed up, too.'

'Suck eggs, Jeffy,' Billy sneered. 'I guess you'll just have to pretend.'

Jeffrey flushed a deep red; he hated Billy at that moment. If he could have made him go home now, he would have, but the other kids would kill him. They were all having heaps of fun. He shoved the Luger deep into his pocket.

'Right, time for the war to begin. My men will wait at the front gate for exactly three minutes. Your men will go to the far side of the property, below the tennis court. There's some scrub down there.'

Billy turned and headed towards the gate. His men fell in behind him, laughing and shouting. The terrier ran alongside Billy like a little snapping shadow.

Jeffrey looked at his watch. Three minutes wasn't long; they needed to hurry. 'Let's go!' he shouted.

They ran across the lawn and down towards the tennis court. By the time they reached the swimming pool, Sam was totally out of breath.

'I have to sit down a sec, I've got a stitch.'

'Get up, Sam,' Jeffrey pleaded.

'I can't, I'm stuffed, I'll get up when I hear them coming.' Sam reached into his shorts pocket and pulled out a Mars Bar, squashy from the heat.

'Come on, Jeff, we better get going or they'll get us too.' Landon looked nervous.

Jeffrey lunged at the Mars Bar and snatched it out of Sam's hand then ran towards the tennis court waving it in the air.

'Oiy, give it back, it's mine!'

'Come and get it, Sam,' Jeffrey shouted.

'Don't have to, I've got another one.' Sam triumphantly hooked the second bar out of his pocket. 'You better not eat that one, Jeffrey. I want it when I get there.'

As Jeffrey and Landon disappeared over the edge of the garden, Billy, Allen and David burst out of the bushes, guns blazing, the blanks loud and convincing.

'You're dead, slowcoach. Out of the game,' Billy jeered.

'No way! I get five minutes, that's the rules, you said.'

'Oh, didn't I mention that if all three of us get you at once, you're out? It must have slipped my mind. Get going. You're our prisoner. You have to do as I say, and I say run.'

Sam stumbled to his feet. The terrier ran barking and nipping at his ankles. At the next turn in the path they caught Landon, frozen like a rabbit in a spotlight. He had stopped to tie his shoelaces. The dog rushed him and knocked him over.

'Hey, bowled by a three-kilo dog, Landon, how do you feel?' Billy was ecstatic. The game would soon be his. Landon joined Sam, hands on his head.

'He's close, I bet. He's right here somewhere.' Billy's voice was a whisper about a metre from Jeffrey's head.

'You go around there, you go over there. You two prisoners stay where you are, and don't move. I'll leave the dog here in case you get any funny ideas.' Billy inched forward on the path, he was right in front of Jeffrey now. Jeffrey felt for the Luger in his pocket. It slipped noiselessly into his hand and he readied himself to spring.

'Aacck aaack aaack aaack.' He leaped out of the bush with the gun drawn. 'Got you, you're dead. I'm taking my men back.'

'No way! I got you first!' Billy screamed. The dog started to bark furiously.

'You're dead!'

'Hey, he's our prisoner now, all three of us got him.' Landon rushed at Billy and tackled him. Sam sat on him while Jeffrey danced about wildly. Allen and David ran back around the path and collided with the rest of them, and in a moment Sam and Landon and Jeffrey were in control.

'We won, we won!' Sam screamed. 'You're the losers, we won!'

'You cheats!' Billy struggled to his feet. His legs were scraped and his shorts were torn.

'Look what you did. You've had it now. I'm going to tell your mum you've been playing with guns!'

He grabbed for the gun in Jeffrey's hand. 'Give me back my guns, all of you, I'm going home. I'll show my father what you did.' The dog was barking and snapping at the air.

'Dob all you like, I don't care. I'm keeping it. And don't forget, losers get executed.' Jeffrey yanked hard. Billy was caught off guard. The gun slipped out of Jeffrey's hand and bounced hard on the concrete path. It flew in the air for a moment—silent—then landed again with a heavy smack of steel. The noise was incredible. Their ears rang with the explosion. A bullet shot out of the barrel straight at the terrier and the dog blew up in mid-bark. Every shrub and tree in a five-metre radius was splattered.

'Jeezus! That thing was loaded!' Sam shook so hard he wobbled.

Jeffrey felt his heart race. He had been playing with a loaded gun! He had run across his garden with a loaded gun in his pocket! He felt sick.

Landon scrambled to the top of the rise. 'It's the police! Hey, it's the police!'

The babysitter and the police arrived together. She had

called them at the first sound of the blanks going off. She knew she would never work here again.

The police eyed the bloody remains in the bushes and the frightened boys in front of them.

'I hope that's not one of your little soldiers sprayed all over the garden.'

Jeffrey's teeth started to chatter. It had been so close.

'Playing with real, loaded guns are we?'

'It's a replica, it can't fire real bullets.' Billy shouted. He began to blubber. His nose ran and he didn't wipe it. 'I didn't know it was real, my dad never said.' His crying got louder and louder.

'Might be an idea for us to go and have a little chat with your dad.' The police officer looked at the others. 'You lot had better go on home to your mothers.'

Billy was marched across the lawn and bundled into the police car. The boys could hear him crying before the car accelerated away.

They stood silently for a moment looking after the car.

'I bet he wishes he had a mother,' Jeffrey said.

Two dead funny books
not to miss

Dead Meat!
Moya Simons

How can anyone accidentally lose
his baby sister?

What does a kid do when his parents freak
out and decide to chain themselves to a tree?

What would it be like to trade your sister
with your friend's sister?

Danny finds out all this and more in this
hilarious book about life, girls, zits-
and other things that matter.

ISBN: 1 86039 059 5

Dead Average!
Moya Simons

*"WANTED. Boy aged about twelve to star
in a TV commercial. Excellent rates of pay.
Must be boy-next-door type. Average looks.
Acting ability essential."*

There are no two ways about it,
Danny is a dead average kid: average hair,
average nose, average eyes, and average freckles.
But landing the starring role in
a TV commercial turns out to be not quite
as wonderful as it sounds!

ISBN: 1 86039 060 9